The V.I.B.s

The Very Important Bees
by
Sabine Muir

Illustrated by Agnieszka Brozek

For Awa, and in memory of Idris, with love

Many thanks to my daughter Amy
for all her help

Copyright © 2020 Sabine Muir

Printed in the United Kingdom
First Printing, 2020

ISBN 978-1-8380125-2-6
Book design by Cat Houston
Myriad Pro Publishing

Beatrice Fraser visits her Granny every day after school while her parents are at work.

She lives at Number 33, Primrose Gardens.

It's a lovely street with pretty gardens full of colourful flowers. The prettiest garden belongs to Granny Fraser.

'Can I watch TV, Granny?'
'Yes, sweetheart, but not for too long
or you'll go square eyed.'

Beatrice noticed a bee dancing on the windowsill.
It buzzed off and dived into a foxglove headfirst.
'Help, help. I'm stuck!' it called out.

Two other bees came to the rescue and
pulled him out. The bee was dizzy as it
came up for air.

The bees were busy tasting nectar from every flower in the garden. There were lupins, roses, pansies, sweet peas, honeysuckle and sunflowers: so much choice for them. A bumble bee flew in through the open window.

'Oh, go away!' Beatrice jumped up and flapped her hands about.

Granny came through with some home-made pancakes.

'Stay still. Don't fuss. It won't do you any harm,' she said.

Granny was right. The bee buzzed back out of the window. Beatrice put some honey on her pancakes and tucked in.

'Thank you, Granny. These are yummy.'

'Let's go to the library after. We need to return your books and choose some new ones,' Granny suggested.

'Oh, yes. I like it when the librarian lets me scan my own books.' said Beatrice.

They found a cosy corner to sit and read.

'Here's a book about bees,' Beatrice said.

She opened it and they read it together. 'I didn't know bees help flowers grow.'

'Yes, bees are very special. It's called pollination,' Granny said. 'They help us grow fruit and vegetables too.'

As they walked back home, they noticed a delivery van
stop at Number One, Primrose Gardens.
Jim from Number One was working in the garden.
'Hi Jim, what's in the box?' asked Nigel from Number Three.

'I'm getting a new 43-inch TV,' Jim said.

'Wow. I always fancied one of those myself,' said Nigel.

'I'm going to dig up the lawn to put down gravel.' said Jim. 'I want a low-maintenance garden. No more Saturday mornings wasted mowing the lawn. Now I'll have more time to watch my fancy new TV.'

Granny tutted. 'You'll go square-eyed.'

'A low-maintenance garden, what an excellent idea,' said Nigel. 'I think I'll do the same.'

Granny frowned.

Awa and Idris from Number 23 were playing outside.

'Do you want to play with us?' Awa asked.

Beatrice turned to Granny, who nodded.

'Yes, OK,' Beatrice said.

The next day Beatrice and her granny walked past Nigel's house. A big van drew up outside his house and two men came up the drive carrying an enormous box.

'What's in the box, Nigel?' Beatrice asked.

'I couldn't resist getting a new 50-inch TV. It is bigger and better than Jim's. No more gardening. I'll have more time to watch TV and play with my Xbox.'

Granny tutted. 'You'll go square-eyed'.

Sheila from Number Five turned her garden into gravel too. She put some plastic flowers in her planter. A bee dived into it. 'Yuk! Plastic flowers... are you kidding me?' the bee said.

Yuk!

Sheila had a 55-inch TV delivered the next day.
'It's bigger and better than Nigel's. I'll have more time to watch TV, play with my Xbox and new phone.'
Granny tutted. 'You'll go square-eyed'.

As the weeks went by the neighbours copied each other
and no-one planted any flowers.
Primrose Gardens looked drab and grey, apart from
Granny Fraser's house, where all the bees gathered.

Beatrice sat in the garden and looked sad. 'None of my friends want to go out to play. They're all watching TV and playing on their devices and phones.

'You were right, Granny. Everyone's gone square eyed.'

She watched Jonathan from Number 15 walking along, looking at his phone.

He walked into a lamppost and fell on his bottom.

Dogs looked depressed gazing from windows, as they were no longer taken for long walks.

Beatrice watched the bees queue up to drink the nectar from the flowers. They bumped into each other.

She listened to what they were saying.

'Hey, it's my turn. You've had long enough,' said one.

Another bee said: 'I've been waiting for ages. Dying of thirst here.'

Another one said: 'I saw that flower first,' and: 'Oh look, Izzy has fainted.'

A bee was lying on the ground. Beatrice carefully picked it up with a tissue and took it inside. 'Granny, can I give it some sugared water? I read in the library book that it rescues them.'

'Yes,' said Granny, 'Wonderful idea.'

'She gave the bee a drink and set the cup by the open window. Once it had recovered, it flew off.

Granny smiled. 'I'm so proud of you, Bea. You did the right thing. If only other people would realize how special bees are.'

'Yes, they are VIPs,' Beatrice said, 'or better still: VI-Bees.'

Granny smiled. 'Yes, absolutely.'

'The bees need more flowers, Granny.'

Beatrice had an idea. She'd seen a recipe for seed bombs in her library book.

'Ding Dong', the doorbell went.

Awa and Idris stood at the door.

'Are you coming out to play?' Idris asked.

'Mum told us to get some fresh air,' Awa added.

'I need your help', Beatrice said. 'Would you like to help me make some seed bombs?'

Awa and Idris nodded.

They went to the shed and gathered all they needed.

The children made lots and lots of seed bombs.

They went around the village...

and threw seed bombs...

into all the gardens.

Soon the entire street was in bloom again.

Jim and Nigel and Sheila waddled outside. They had put on lots of weight. Nigel scratched his head. 'Where did the flowers come from?'

'I've no idea, but they're nice,' Sheila said, 'Let's sit outside and enjoy them.'

Soon everyone in the street got fed up sitting on their couches getting fatter. They started gardening again.

Later that summer, Awa, Idris and Beatrice won awards from the Horticultural Society. It was for bringing beautiful flowers back to the village. Granny got an award for the most beautiful garden.

Miss Petunia Greensleeves, the president of the society, said: 'We've also got a special award, which goes to Beatrice, for opening our eyes to how important bees are. Well done to our very own VI-Bea.'

Everyone clapped. Granny was proud of the children.

'Come, let's go home,' she said.

'Did you know that a bee produces a teaspoon of honey in its lifetime?' Beatrice said.

'No, but I do now.' Granny winked as she put a teaspoon of honey on Beatrice's pancakes.

A bee landed on her shoulder.

'Thank you for the honey,' Beatrice said.

'You're welcome,' the bee whispered in her ear. 'Thank you for the flowers.'

~ The End ~

Seed Bomb Recipe
You will need:

Flower seeds from a shop (meadow mix) or seeds collected from the garden

Peat-free compost

Powdered clay (from craft shops)

...and water

In a large bowl, mix 1 cup of seeds with 5 cups of compost and 2-3 cups of clay powder.

Add some water and slowly mix together with your hands until everything sticks together.

Roll the mixture into firm balls.

Leave the balls to dry in a sunny spot.

Plant your seed bombs by throwing them at bare parts of the garden and wait to see what pops up.